When Rosie l

Steve Wilson

Illustrations by *Jacinthe Betts*

To Chris and Rich.

Long Mynd Memorial
Soc!

All the best

Steve

Rosie

Panther Publishing

2/5/07

First Published by Panther Publishing Ltd in 2002
Panther Publishing Ltd, 10 Lime Avenue, High Wycombe, Bucks HP11 1DP, UK

Acknowledgements
This book was written with love for the real Rosie. And for her mother.

With thanks also to Mick Coombes and Andy Williams for technical assistance, to Nick Ward for tractor input, to Ruth de Wilton for local knowledge, to Jacinthe Betts for the illustrations - and to Rosie again, for reminding me how many sides the Church tower has! And finally to Pantherman Rollo, for making it all happen.

Illustrations
The illustrations depicting Celtic designs were inspired by the Book of Kells and the Lindisfarne manuscripts.

ISBN 09535098 4 2

Rosie ran into the wind after the dog, down the tilting grass slope, ran so fast that her fair hair flew straight out behind her. Ahead Zoe the black dog was running so hard her ears were streaming, her paws scarcely touching the ground.

It was a bright spring morning, one of the first, a morning when you could forget all your troubles, a morning when anything seemed possible. The horses in the field watched with their ears pricked as Rosie and the black Labrador pelted down the wet tussocky grass and skidded to a halt by the five-bar gate. Rosie picked her way around the squelchy hoof-churned mud, which wanted to suck her rubber boots from her feet. She opened the gate for Zoe, closed it again carefully still standing on the near side, and then clambered over the tall gate just for the fun of it.

The second field sloped down steadily for a quarter of a mile to the hollow at the far end, and a fence beside a tumbledown barn. From there, a tilting ploughed field rose steadily to the line of the road. Cross that, and the steep slopes with the tracks of the racehorse gallops led up the hill to the Ridgeway path that ran along the top. Turn right on the Ridgeway, and a mile further west the track took you up behind the big circle of the Iron Age fort that had stood on the highest point of the hill. Beyond that lay the White Horse itself, the figure that had been carved into the far slope, Rosie's

Dad had told her, three thousand years ago. That was the way Rosie and Zoe were going.

The dog was off already, nose to the ground, running down the next field on the trail of a rabbit. She was probably following the scent the wrong way, as usual, because Rosie knew that the rabbit's burrows were all uphill, in the bank under the hedge above her . The labrador never caught anything she chased – she was not a hunting dog, but a retriever, Mum had explained, and once Zoe had actually brought them back a live, flustered pheasant in her soft mouth, for them to release. But she did love to chase the smells.

Rosie let her go – she'd be back soon enough, she wasn't a dog that went off – and angled up the big field to the top hedge. The thing everyone knew about Rosie was that she had very sharp eyes. And that she loved the world of nature. Years ago she had surprised her mother by telling her that a wood-louse in her play-house was having babies, a double surprise when the tiny globes suspended beneath the armoured insect, itself no bigger than a pea, *had* turned out to be its young. She loved to dig in the hill of soil behind their cottage, spotting and saving pottery fragments and other treasures from the ancient rubbish tip, which pleased her father, who did work like that for a living.

Now Rosie scanned the rabbit diggings to see which were fresh and where the droppings lay. She bent to gaze at the yellow cowslips under the hedge. Then, shading her eyes against the rising sun, she peered into the hedge itself. Sure enough, a little way along, there was a bird's nest. Zoe trotted back panting, her tongue lolling, as Rosie carefully eased herself in, the brambles scratching at her green thornproof coat, and peered into the nest. No, no eggs, it was an abandoned one from last year. She pulled it out and looked down at the bundle of twigs and moss, and the few downy feathers which clung to the inside. Rosie's mind could be as dreamy as her eyes were sharp, and for long moments she stood staring at the empty home in her hands.

Then she dropped it on the ground. And as if a gun had gone off, a young rabbit streaked from where it had been crouched under the hedge, ran almost between Rosie's legs, and bolted off under the dog's nose flat out downhill. Even Zoe could not miss this one and she tore off in hot pursuit, with Rosie running after.

They raced down the field, Zoe less than ten feet from the rabbit's white bobtail, not gaining ground but not losing any either, with Rosie trailing behind. At the far end of the field the rabbit sprinted under the fence, angled right and disappeared into the old barn, with the black dog crashing through the tangled undergrowth and plunging after it and out of sight.

Rosie stopped, her chest heaving and her lungs burning painfully from the hard run. Straight in front of her was the collapsed barn, which lay in a dip, its dark bulk, as tall as a three storey house, tilted down at the far end like a ship sinking, the outline disappearing into newly budding willow trees. The barn's high, steeply canted roof made of streaked corrugated iron which rust had painted a bright orangey brown came right down to the ground on the side where Rosie stood. There was something sombre, sinister even, about the foundering building. Ever since she had been allowed to walk the dog on her own, Rosie had skirted the place with scarcely a look, walking on up to the Ridgeway. She had to look at it now.

And there was more. As she stopped for a moment gazing at the huge barn,

catching her breath, waiting to see if Zoe would give up and trot back out to her, she felt something else. The brisk wind was still whipping in hard from the west, but what she felt was something like the way, on a warm summer's afternoon, when you look down a road or into the distance, the heat makes everything waver before your eyes. Things seemed to shimmer slightly, yet to be very still. Afterwards she would turn it over endlessly in her mind – had she felt that something very unusual was just about to happen to her?

What she always ended up believing was that it had been even more than that. Her heart was pounding, and not just from the running. Like polished metal gleaming once as a beam of sunlight struck it, something was coming: it might be terror or delight, but something inside her told her that neither were the point, that she was standing at the gateway to a place where there lived presences, forces, patterns and tales older than you could begin to imagine, yet more real than the sunny field where she stood now, stock still.

Then from inside the barn Rosie heard Zoe's yelp. Her dog might be in trouble, and she moved.

R osie clambered through the tall fence and picked her way round to the eastern end of the building. This was made of big overlapping planks of wood, but the barn's fall, and the time which had passed since then, meant that several sections of the planking had fallen away, and with the shafts of sunlight that shone through the gaps into the barn's interior, Rosie could see inside a little.

Nothing was moving in there. She called Zoe, but there was no reply. She moved forward gingerly. The brown barn was surrounded by tall, untrimmed bushes, some just budding, and by a chaos of fallen planks, set in a tangle of pale, matted dead grass, big brambles and catkins, all yellowy white in contrast to the green of the fields she was leaving.

Rosie was bold, but by the time she had struggled round the corner of the barn to its second long side, the choking, unkempt vegetation was above her head. She also found that she had to be careful of hidden, rusted metal things in the undergrowth, old farm machines or bits of them, concealed within the tangle and waiting to trip her up or cut her legs. She inched her way carefully through the thorny jungle, eyes down and hands held up at shoulder level to avoid the spikes, following a faint animal trail through the chaos. Long, dead brambles studded with thorns had woven themselves into the withered stalks and whippy branches to make something like a spider-web, thought Rosie, a

spider-web with teeth; and she was the fly. But she pushed firmly on.

The southern side of the barn had been open, with the lower, lengthways beam for the sloping roof above propped up on thick wooden posts, now weathered pale grey. But half way along, something had pushed the big posts over, snapping one like a twig so that the whole barn had subsided crazily and the far end collapsed into the dip.

The faint track Rosie was following led into the barn at that broken point, where the rust-brown iron roof sagged low to the ground. She found herself brushing by a rusted metal cartwheel almost as tall as she was, sunk in the weeds. Attached to it somehow, and well above her head there reared, with branches looping around it, a metal saddle with holes in it, like the one on the old grey tractor she knew from the Farm Shop playground. It was like a war, she thought, as if a shell had hit the building, and then the fighting had moved on, leaving everything abandoned. She peered into the darkness of the barn and again called Zoe's name. When there was no answer, she stepped out of the sunlight and entered the shadows inside.

The place smelled of cold, damp earth, and its floor was as jumbled as the undergrowth surrounding it, but in a different way. Planks, poles, roof timbers and sheets of corrugated iron at crazy angles made walking just as difficult as outside, and perhaps more dangerous. As her eyes became accustomed to the gloom, shot through with blinding shafts of light where there were chinks in the wall or timbers missing, Rosie saw that the whole huge roof where it had fallen was only held up in places by wooden posts now tilted at crazy angles, and resting on the same unsteady jumble of planks and rubble which she was picking her way across. One wrong move could bring it all down. Her heart beat hard, and she breathed the earth-smelling air in through an open mouth. But it only made her more determined to find the dog.

After looking around, carefully she made her way, wobbling and slipping on the heaped timber and rubbish, towards the tumbledown end of the barn. As she moved nearer to it, she thought she could make out a still darker space at the very far end. Picking past great tumbled sections taller than herself, ducking her head round pale beams lying at an angle and over the broken planks between them, she gradually realised that a curtain of fallen corrugated iron masked a further enclosed space between where the worst fall had happened, and the end wall of the barn. There was no way a grown person could reach this hidden inner space. But a dog could. Or a child.

Rosie got on her hands and knees, wincing as a splinter dug into her left palm. But she had to go on, as from within the inner place she thought she had heard scuffling and a whimper. Rosie shouldered and slid her way into the dark interior, where she could stand up again.

Suddenly she jerked with fright, as in the dark, something brushed against her outstretched hand. She squeaked, but then a familiar rhythmic thumping against a fallen plank, and a cold wet nose thrust in her palm, told her that she had found Zoe, and that the dog was wagging its tail in delight. The feel of earth on Zoe's muzzle suggested that she had been rooting about, no doubt after the rabbit.

"What've you found, Zo?" she half-whispered, and the thumping quickened as the big black dog beat her tail in a frenzy. Zoe scuffled and pawed again at something in the far corner of the secret space. As Rosie's eyes grew accustomed to the faint light which filtered through a few small gaps in the planks of the far wall, she could make out the dark bulk of something leaning in the corner, with a covering over it at which Zoe was pawing.

Rosie stepped over and heaved the cover away. Her first reaction was slight disappointment. Underneath was just another piece of old machinery. In this case, she discovered, a dirty old motorbike. With flat tyres, a smashed headlamp where a roof beam had hit it, and all covered in oil and dust. Though when Rosie pulled back the cover, which turned out to be a massive, stiff old riding coat that she could barely lift, when the front end was exposed, something had gleamed at her as a shaft of light fell on the uncovered tank. Most of the tank was dusted in light rust, but beneath that there was a silvery brightness.

Rosie looked closer, and on the side of the tank made out a metal badge. She bent forward to see what it said, and made out a 'B' with a wing streaming back from it, followed by an 'S' and an 'A'. Rosie's interest quickened. On the sitting room wall of their cottage, there hung a blown-up old black and white photo of her Dad when he was young smiling at the camera as he sat astride a motorbike. And Rosie's sharp eyes had often noticed the letters on its tank, the same winged letters: 'BSA'.

Dad will be interested in this, she thought, tugging back the dusty greatcoat further. As the seat was exposed, she found that sitting on it, concealed under the coat, was an old silver crash helmet, like an upside-down pudding basin. Rosie reached out and picked

it up,
looking
inside   for
spiders. Finding none in
the leather and webbing straps, for a laugh she put the helmet on.
And a voice in her ears said
    "Bloimey! What took you so long?"

R osie jumped, snatching off the helmet and staring wildly around her into the gloom. But in the still, dusty, cave-like space, all was silent, nothing moved. After that she peered into the helmet to see if there were headphones there, like the ones on her Walkman. But there were only old webbing straps. Gingerly, she lowered the helmet back onto her head.

"Wassermarrer?" said the voice. "Oi wunt hurt yow."

"Who are you?" wavered Rosie.

"Packirin!" said the voice scornfully.

"Are you…are you the motorbike?" said Rosie in disbelief.

"Croiky," said the strange voice, "yow talk with a quid in yer gob. Course oim the mowta boik. A BSA," it announced proudly. "From Brumijem."

Somehow Rosie realised that it meant Birmingham. The voice sounded something like the one her father used to put on when he was reading the part of Eeyore in Pooh Bear stories. Doleful, but also strong and mischievous, as if the speaker was laughing at you from behind a mask of gloom. Having to work out what it was saying helped take Rosie's mind off the very odd thought that she might actually be having a conversation with a motorbike. As they carried on, she found that she could make out its words more clearly.

"How long have you been here?" she asked.

"Oi dunno" said the BSA. "A long toime. Check me tax disc. In the little glass bit down by mi front wheel."

Rosie bent down in the gloom, and after a bit found the tax disc holder. With a tissue from her pocket she cleaned off the glass, and then straightened up slowly.

"'Smarra?" said the voice.

"It said…1958," replied Rosie. She couldn't quite do the exact sum, but finally said, "I think you've been here more than forty years."

"Yuwa?" said the voice sharply. "Gerraway!"

"I'm sorry," said Rosie softly, "but I think it's true. How did you come to get left here? Did someone forget about you?"

"Forty bloomin' years," said the voice gloomily. "No, oi dunno what happened, rilly. Me gaffer the farmer rode me in here one morning, then wint out to the tractow. It were a voyal great green thing, that tractow. Oim 650cc with two cylinders, miself, but it only had the one cylinder and it said it was 4,000cc! With just one great big, great big piston. And a chimney on top of her loik the Queen Mary!

"Naow the gaffer, the farmer, was ownly a little bloke, bandy-legged, loik – he couldn't stop a pig in a gateway. Oi heard him trying to start the tractow, which was not summat you'd want to do twice in one day. Sometimes he'd use a roight big starting handle he kept behind the seat, and sometimes he'd stick a lit starting paper in the front end, and fire off a bloomin' cartridge – no, sroit thou!

"Anyroad, oi hear the brute fire up, and oi hear the owd gaffer yell, and the next thing oi now, the roof fell in on me, literal loik. Smashed me headlamp. The tractow had ploughed into the barn!

"Oi think the owd man was all roit, oi heard him talking a bit after that when they took the tractow away. But he never come for me. Just left me here to rot," said the voice, in genuine sorrow.

"Oi never did him any harm, even thou he weren't the best roider in the world. Just left me…"

"What have you been doing?" asked Rosie gently, wondering quite what it would have been like to have been left alone for over forty years, especially if you'd been born to run.

"Nowt," said the BSA. "Big sleep, rilly. There was the spoiders, o' course. And families of moice used to nest in mi pipes, till the silencers rotted away…I suppose I'm just scrap, now," the voice continued dolefully. "Forty years owd - that's Obsolete. Obsolete four times over…"

"No, no," said Rosie determinedly, "lots of people are interested in old machines, honestly. My Dad…my Dad had a BSA once! And I know he'd love to have one again." Rosie couldn't bear to see anything upset, even a motorbike, if there was something she could do about it. And she also loved to make plans and schemes.

"Listen," she went on excitedly, "the first thing to do is find out where you came from, and whether they'd let us have you. Which direction was the farm?"

"Oop the hill and along the road to the roit," said the voice despondently. "But oi dunno, ar kid. The gaffer must be long gone, binow."

"Yes," said Rosie, "but I know that farm! In the summer my Mum helps them with the cream teas they do, sometimes. And it's the same family! The lady who runs it, Mrs Honeywell, her father had it before her, she said. Her husband died, and she runs the farm on her own now, and she's very nice." Then Rosie thought for a moment. "Tell me – did you talk to the farmer, like this?"

"'im? Naow. Oi never talked to a person before – leastways they never heard me. You must be something special, ar kid. To have the ears to hear. And now to be taking trouble over a rusty owd heap like me."

"Nonsense," said Rosie briskly, "we'll have you like new again in no time. Now I'll have to leave you for a bit. Shall I put the coat back over you?"

"Yes pliz," said the voice. "Oi'd be a lot worse off if the gaffer hadn't throwed his owd footing coat over me that morning."

" 'Footing coat'?" asked Rosie, as she moved Zoe off the coat where the dog had settled down comfortably.

"In competition, in Trials on the dirt," the bike explained, "when you touched the ground, what they called 'footed', you lost a point. But some of these coats were that long, you could dab your foot down for a second to steady y'self, and no one would see! 'Footing coat,' roit? Here, ar kid, fore you take the helmet off – what's yer name?"

"Rosie, Rosie Ransom," she said. "What's yours?"

"Well they called us 650s 'Golden Flashes' because of our colour, though my paint was to special order – it's mostly red – or it was. I can tell you my engine number – CA1010593. But I ain't gorra name of me own. Anyroad, noice to meetcha, Rosie. Mek haste and come back now. Tara..." as Rosie gently pulled off the helmet.

"Tara," mouthed Rosie, and then as she pulled the coat back into place, she noticed the grubby white registration letters neatly painted on the bike's rear number plate. They read: ANN 911.

"You have got a name," whispered Rosie. "Or at least you will have."

Back in the light, Rosie, full of purpose now, fought her way out of the brambles, climbed another wooden gate, and set off up hill along the edge of a ploughed field, climbing towards the road. When she reached the highway she called Zoe, gave her a biscuit for coming promptly, and put her on the lead. Then they started off carefully westwards, into the wind. Rosie walked along the right side of the narrow road, facing the oncoming traffic. There were not many cars that morning but they came quickly, swerving to miss her, as it was, she guessed by the sun behind her, going-to-work time.

To her left, the slopes of the Downs rose smoothly, with the darker wood-chip surface of the Gallops, where the racehorses trained in all weathers, turning to run straight up the hill. And as Rosie went on, a line of horses came up from behind her on the other side of the hedge across the road, the slight figures of the lads and girls, in hard hats and coloured jackets, hunched high up on the tall, highly strung and beautiful horses. They sat in their saddles with an utter confidence Rosie could only envy, some puffing on cigarettes and others chattering to each other. One of the girls, a neighbour's daughter, called hallo to Rosie, and one of the lads looked at Zoe and said "Good pup!" which even though Zoe was five years old, put a spring in her step as she trotted along the road, nails clicking. Then the line turned onto the uphill gallop and were off, pounding away up the slope, tails flying, muscle and sinew bunching and stretching as they flew away up the hill.

Rosie stood watching till they had galloped to the distant top, the Ridgeway path. Horses everywhere round here, she thought; it was one reason she never wanted to live anywhere else. There were the thoroughbreds from the racing yards. And there were the ponies at the riding stables where she went once a fortnight, including her favourite, Winnie, even though he was naughty and had a belly like a barrel. A pony of her own was an impossible dream, she knew, because they couldn't afford it. And always there was the White Horse, just on the other side of some woods, a chalk outline tilted upwards across the top of a steep slope, pointing to open uplands. She could feel it now, even though it was hidden behind the wooded slope in the distance ahead. The Horse, she often thought, for such a big and magnificent creation, was curiously evasive, shy about being seen. There were very few places from which you could view it whole. The Horse was, she felt sure, part of a story, a tale where the beginning and end had been lost, a story which you could spend your whole life puzzling out.

That, she thought, was just about what her father was doing. And, she sighed to herself, he was stuck.

Then she had to pay strict attention as the road went down and up and down again, twisting sharply around the base of first one coombe and then another, with a car or two coming at them out of nowhere, so that Zoe cowered away. The road was fringed with tall bushes, their tops completely covered in hanging white foliage, wispy and frothing, which her mother had told her was called Old Man's Beard. It was amazing, covering the bushes as snow covers pine trees and dangling down, and its strange beauty made Rosie forget about her sore feet in their muddy boots. Soon they rounded a last bend, and there was the field with the caravan in it, beside the old woods which arced in a horseshoe up around the farm.

Rosie and Zoe turned through the gates and trudged up the muddy track, past big open modern barns, Rosie feeling

increasingly uncertain about what she was going to say. Certainly nothing about talking motorbikes! Then as they approached the white-painted farmhouse, suddenly a thickset black and white sheepdog appeared and sprang at them, barking furiously. Zoe was no fighter, but the hair along her spine puffed out as her hackles rose instinctively and growling, she nearly pulled Rosie over.

The farm door opened and a woman's voice called sharply "Shep! Be quiet! Go on!" The dog turned to her as Mrs Honeywell stepped out to see what all the fuss was about.

"Hullo, Rosie!" she said in surprise. "What are you doing up here? If you've come to see the boys, I'm afraid they're off with their Uncle, helping with the lambs." The sheep from the farm grazed the slopes of White Horse Hill, and below it the flat valley with the wonderful waving edges which they called the Manger. Lorna Honeywell's younger sons went to the village school with

Rosie, though they were older than her and not particular friends.

"No," said Rosie, "it's not that, I was just taking Zoe for a walk, and I – found something, and I'd like to talk to you about it. Please," she remembered to add.

Mrs Honeywell looked at her more closely. "How far have you come?" she asked. "A fair way, by the look of you. I expect your Mum will be wondering where you've got to," she went on. "Have you had your breakfast yet?"

"No," said Rosie, "I always have it when I get back."

"Well that'll be a while now, you're a mile or two from home, and it's half past nine already. I'll tell you what. You come inside and we'll phone your Mum to let her know you're all right. Then you can have some breakfast with me, I was up with the lambs half the night, and I'm just putting mine on. And you can tell me all about it while we're having a bite to eat. All right?"

Lorna Honeywell had brown hair, a pretty face round as the moon, big brown eyes that stuck out a little bit, like a rabbit's, and a comfortable figure. Her manner was direct but her voice talking to Rosie was soft, and Rosie didn't hesitate.

"Thank you, Mrs Honeywell," she said gratefully, for she had just realised, first, that her Mum might be worrying, and second, that she was very hungry indeed. Zoe was too muddy to come into the house so they tied her up by her lead in the porch near a bowl of water, and after Rosie had given the dog a couple of biscuits, and Mrs Honeywell had assured her that Shep wouldn't be a bother, they entered the farm.

After the wind outdoors which never really ceased, the farm kitchen was snug and warm, with a tiny lamb curled up in a wooden box beside the old cream-coloured Raeburn stove. They had phoned Rosie's Mum and reassured her, and Mrs Honeywell was cracking the farm's own brown eggs into a frying pan on the top of the stove in which bacon already sizzled, as she explained that the lamb was one that had got separated from its mother, and was there for her to feed from a bottle.

"I've been doing that since the mornings before I used to go down to school in the village, when I was your age and younger. With my Dad Wilf, the rule was always, the animals before us. Here, have a cup of tea."

Rosie knew the village was about a mile and a half away from the farm, and asked "How did you used to get to school, Mrs Honeywell?"

"Call me Lorna. Sometimes I roller-skated. By the bottom of that hill below the cross-roads leading up to the Horse, I'd have red hot wheels!" She opened the oven door and pulled out warm Willow Pattern plates, and toast clamped in a wire rack. Soon they were feasting on big platefuls of bacon and egg. Only when their plates were clean did the farm lady ask

"Now, what was it that you found, Rosie?"

So Rosie told her the whole story, except the bit about the talking helmet. When she was done, Mrs Honeywell laughed.

"Well, the motorbike! I always thought my Dad had sold it on, but he must have just left it there after the accident he had down there. You see, after that Dad wouldn't have anything to do with machinery any more - any machinery. Do you know what happened to the barn?"

"No-oo," said Rosie carefully.

"Well I'll tell you the whole story," said Mrs Honeywell, "but to understand it properly, first you have to know about my Dad, Wilf. He wasn't from round here. He was brought in by Sir Peter Astley, the gentleman who owned the farm then. This was in the hard times before the last war, after the farm's previous tenants had simply walked off the land and left.

"Dad had grown up farming in Norfolk, and he'd say about this place, 'whenever you go out of the door here, you're on a hill.' And he wasn't used to the hills. And the land here was different too, the mix of clay and chalk. The cornfield up the hill behind the wood is very steep, with the land curving. In the early days he would work it with plough horses, but after the war he knew he should use machinery, as everyone was beginning to do. But because of the hills there was always the safety worry of tipping over. The tractors were much lighter then.

"So when he could afford it, because we'd done quite well, my Dad Wilf decided that he'd get the heaviest and best tractor that money could buy. He'd been in touch with his old pals in Norfolk, and they'd told him that the thing to go for was something called a Field Marshall. 'The Rolls-Royce of tractors,' said Dad. 'That'll pull like a steam train'. It wasn't as big as the tractors are now of course, but to us it seemed an enormous thing, dark green with silver wheels and a great black funnel running up one side" (*'Like the Queen Mary,'* Rosie thought to herself). Not very long, but massive – and loud? The heavens rang!

"And it was a devil, a beast. When he delivered it, the tractor agent wouldn't start it. So Dad quickly found out that to do that, you had to load it with a special 12-bore cartridge, then wad up a sheet of blotting paper soaked in chemicals, light that with a cigarette end, and use a hammer to clout the firing pin and set off the cartridge! Honestly! If it worked, you were then choked with smoke before the thing settled down to its regular shaking and banging. The engine was massive.

"The cartridge didn't always work," Mrs Honeywell continued. "And if it didn't, you had to use the starting handle, which a lot of vehicles had in those days. With this one, you stuck it in the side, into the middle of a great big flywheel – and then you only had about half a dozen turns to get it going.

"Being such a bother to start, one time in the early days he left its engine running, after ploughing in that top field, while he went to fetch something. But its great big piston…" "What's a piston?" asked Rosie. "Ask your Dad," Mrs Honeywell shot back " – anyway, its piston banging backwards and forwards inside meant that the tractor always dithered about at a standstill, and by the time Wilf got back, it had shaken itself down the muddy slope and was just about to topple into the woods!

"That chimney was trouble, too. When it rained and the Field Marshall stood outside, after a bit the water would get down the funnel and into the engine. Then it wouldn't start again. Once Dad got so desperate he had a neighbour on his tractor tow the brute around a field in gear, to try and bump-start it. But the Field Marshall then shot all the water inside it out from its front, just like a giant water pistol, and soaked the neighbour on the towing tractor all down the back of his neck!

"So after that Dad would put an upturned bucket over the top of the chimney to keep the rain out. Until the day he forgot about it, and started the tractor with a cartridge. The engine caught, and fired the bucket up in the air like a rocket! And it nearly brained Dad when it fell to earth again.

"I think the Field Marshall would have been all right on the level. That's why it had been recommended by Dad's friends in Norfolk, which I believe is very flat. Round here, even when it was running, it wasn't always favourite. It's true that it pulled like a train, but because it was so short, going uphill towing a load could make the front wheels lift clear off the ground! I remember one day in the top field, watching Dad at the wheel pulling a loaded muck-spreader uphill at full throttle. The noise was deafening, the front wheels were a foot up pawing the air, the chimney was blowing black smoke rings, and Dad was standing up, his face all dirty with oily smuts, peering desperately through the smoke while the muck-spreader spewed out its load in a fountain behind. It was quite a sight," laughed Mrs Honeywell.

"So the Field Marshall wasn't a great success. But at the same time he got the motorbike, the BSA. His 'Iron Horse', he called it, 'King of the Queen's Highway'. We didn't have a car then, just the old Land Rover, so it was like a treat for Wilf. He had few enough of them, and Mum never minded. It had to be a BSA. Nortons were too expensive, he said, and he considered Triumphs were dainty, lady-like things with no 'bottom'. But he'd heard about BSA army bikes from the boys who'd been away in the war, and he reckoned they were strong. The one he bought, the 650 Golden Flash, was said to be the best, and it did seem solidly built, and never let him down. And it was exceedingly handsome, too. He looked all over till he got one in the colours he wanted, red and chrome. He finally found one, a couple of years old, up Northampton way.

"He skidded off it a couple of times, I believe, before he got the hang, though that wasn't so dangerous then, there wasn't the traffic. But he was proud as anything of that bike. It was hard to keep it nice, up here with the muddy yard, but he did, cleaning it every Sunday."

"Did you used to go on it?" asked Rosie.

"Only the once," laughed Mrs Honeywell. "I was just little then, younger than you, and a bit timid, having only known the farm. He lifted me up onto the tank in front of him, but the noise of the engine scared me too much to enjoy the ride, and it was the same for my brother too. But he'd take my Mum out sometimes, proud as punch, and that was another reason to keep the BSA nice. When the winter was coming, he put thick grease on the wheel rims and the lower engine. That way it wouldn't get rusty, and he could wipe it off again easy enough come Spring.

"But it was that October, ploughing time after harvest, when the accident happened. He'd left the tractor down in the bottom field by the barn that night, so next morning he rode the bike down the track, which is gone now, to the old barn. I can remember Dad pulling away on the BSA, wearing his big old despatch rider's coat…"

"His footing coat," said Rosie before she could stop herself. This earned her a curious look from Mrs Honeywell, which made Rosie blush deep red. But the farm lady knew that Rosie was an only child, with no brothers or sisters, and that from spending so much time with adults, she often came out with unexpectedly grown-up turns of phrase.

"That's right Rosie, he did used to call it that. He was only a short chap and a bit bow-legged from his time as a lad working with the horses, and when he sat on the bike with the coat all buckled up, you couldn't see his feet. Anyway, off he went. When he got to the Field Marshall, he found that he'd run out of starting cartridges, so he fished out the great big starting handle from behind the seat.

"Now as I said, you only had about five twiddles with that starting handle before something happened inside that could make the engine kick back, badly. That's what must have happened, as Dad gave the handle one twirl too many – and that wasn't all.

"He'd left the tractor on the slope above the barn, facing uphill. Now as I told you, the Field Marshal was a real beast and its engine would sometimes run backwards and go into reverse. And that's what happened. The shock of the kickback must have knocked the brute into gear, and it set off running *backwards*, downhill, towards the barn. Dad might have jumped on and stopped it, but then something else happened in the engine, and the starting handle was shot out of the side at him! He had to dive in the mud as the heavy handle whizzed over his head like a boomerang! Dad was terrified, and by the time he got up, it was too late. The Field Marshall had roared backwards downhill and crashed into the barn, knocking out a pillar and collapsing one end like a house of cards. It was a proper smash-up.

"Dad was really badly shaken. That Field Marshall had destroyed all his belief in machinery. He wasn't a great talker so he never said much about it, but from that day on, till five years later when he died, he never again took the wheel of a vehicle. Mum used to drive him anywhere he had to go, in the old Land Rover. And he wouldn't have another piece of motorized machinery on the farm. We went back to doing everything with horses, which at that time on a small farm you still could just about get away with. Haymaking seemed to go on and on, and I'd ride down to the men with hot bottles of tea and sandwiches in a knapsack. Mum was a little nervous of horses, but she still used to ride the great Shires bareback, and we all have very fond memories of the horses.

"I had my pony Silver," – inside herself, Rosie sighed enviously – "and I would exercise her, put her on a lunge rein in the front paddock, where the caravan is now. And tourists would pull up and ask, 'Gee, is that the White Horse?'"

They laughed, and then something, perhaps the memory of that moment standing in front of the old barn, made Rosie ask "Mrs Hon…sorry, Lorna – you've always lived here, close under the Horse, but have you ever felt anything? Or heard anything – my Dad says some people used to think they could hear the old battles being fought, at night?"

Lorna Honeywell thought for a while, and then shook her head. "No, I just feel comfortable, really, with the Horse always being there." Rosie could understand that, and she also nodded when Mrs Honeywell went on, "I used to love standing in the eye of the Horse and wishing. Especially that moment just before you wish." You weren't really supposed to stand in the chalk dot high on the slope that was the Horse's eye, but a lot of people did, Rosie included, after she learned that you could make a true wish on it. Rosie's wish was always the same. She wished she could fly.

"And how's your Dad getting on with his work?" asked Mrs Honeywell. "Is he any closer to an answer?" Most of the local people knew about Professor's Ransom's work on the Horse with the Oxford Archaeological Team, his persistent attempt to uncover its mysteries.

"I'm afraid not," said Rosie. "That's sort of why I was wondering…if we could have the old motorbike," she blurted out, blushing red. "It's just, I mean, it might cheer Dad up a bit, take his mind off his work sometimes…He used to have a BSA, you know …and I'm sure we could pay whatever it's worth…I've saved most of my pocket money…" She broke off, feeling wretched. She shouldn't have asked, she knew now.

"That's a very kind thought, Rosie," said Mrs Honeywell, and after that sat in silence considering carefully for long moments. Then she said, "Actually, I think it's a very good idea. My brother's never had any interest in motorbikes – probably because of that one! My eldest boy Tom is already restoring our old Land Rover, and to be honest I'm not eager for him or the other two to get keen on bikes – there's a lot more traffic everywhere today than there was then, and for young lads it's a bit too dangerous for my liking. But if your Dad knows how to ride already, I'm sure he'll be all right. And I think it would have pleased Wilf, the old BSA going to a good home. That's if you can ever get it running again!" In truth, Mrs Honeywell had always had a soft spot for Rosie's parents, Roderick and Mary Ransom. She was pleased to have an opportunity to do something for them.

"Oh we will get it going!" said Rosie excitedly. "Thank you, thank you so much! I wonder," she went on, "have you got a photo of the bike when it was new, so that my Dad could see how it should look?"

"Good idea," said Lorna Honeywell, going over to a massive black oak dresser. "Now let me see," she said, opening the bottom doors to reveal a vast jumble of papers, bound albums, odds and ends of every sort. She shrugged helplessly. "You see, first Dad died, and then I married Joe, and then we bought the farm off the Astley Estate, and then Mum died, and the National Trust took over White Horse Hill…And then Joe died… and the foot and mouth scare…What I'm trying to say," she went on, rummaging furiously, "is that in forty years I never seem to have had time to tidy out this blooming cupboard!"

Behind her the lamb bleated, disturbed by the activity, and Mrs Honeywell said "Rosie dear, her bottle's on the stove. Be a good girl and…" But Rosie needed no telling, and in an instant the lamb was up on her lap and she was laughing excitedly as it shook and tugged fiercely at the rubber teat on the warm bottle of milk, and Rosie felt the life flowing from it and into it.

"I really enjoy lambing," said Lorna Honeywell, nodding her approval. "The sheep have always been brought into the shed here to be lambed. Bottlers were always the naughtiest, the ones who got out. Half a dozen of them would follow me everywhere. We kids would run races on them…Ah, here it is," she cried, holding up a discoloured cellophane packet. "And look here, you're in luck. There's the picture I remembered, but it's been put away with all the other old bike things." And she showed Rosie a bill of sale for the motorbike, a beige handbook about it from the makers, and a green card booklet that opened out like a concertina. Lorna said that it was the original log book. "And look here, there's a modern one too, what they call a V5. Mum must have sent for it when they changed over from the old kind – she did it for the first Land Rover too, which has pleased my boy Tom a lot, now he's doing it up. I wonder if she knew the bike was still down in the barn? Or whether she did it just to be on the safe side. Well, whatever it was, having that should save you some trouble."

On top of the pile lay the photo, a small black and white print with white edges showing a short, stocky man with Mrs Honeywell's shining eyes, dressed in a big flat cap and an enormous coat, grinning shyly as he stood by a splendidly shiny BSA.

"That was taken the day he got it, I believe," said Mrs Honeywell softly. "He got a crash helmet later, after he'd tumbled off a time or two." Suddenly she came to Rosie's side and hugged her. "I'm sorry," she said huskily. "The picture brought it back. My Dad. And Joe." She sighed once, and went on "It's been five years now he's been gone. The farm in a way has been a godsend. It fills your thoughts, exceedingly…"

Rosie didn't know quite what to say. She kneaded the lamb's thick fur gently and asked, "Can I please come and help you do this again?"

"'Course you can, dear," said Mrs Honeywell warmly. "'Course you can! Now, look here, your Mum will be starting to wonder where we've got to. I'll just get my boots on, and then take you and the dog home in the Land Rover."

A little while later Rosie stood in their cottage, outside the door of her father's study. As she had been taught to do, she knocked before going in. Seated at his cluttered desk, her father looked up with his usual mixture of bemusement, irritation, and pleasure at seeing her.

Rosie stepped inside. Encircling her, all around the sloping walls of the beamed attic room, were blown-up reproductions of intricate, curving black patterns, Celtic designs from around the time when the Horse had been made. There were shapes and faces within the patterns, fantastical creatures, part animal, part man. Or dragons' heads rearing back to confront one another on powerful curves of an absolute grace and authority. It was a flowing world of dreams, dreams  which could turn into nightmares, and she knew it was the world within which her father lived.

"Daddy," said Rosie excitedly, "I've got something to tell you…"

"Just have a look at this first, darling," her father cut in. He held up another large blown-up black and white photo, the White Horse itself, seen from the air. Rosie was very familiar with its strange, lovely white shape. It was even on the front of her green school uniform sweater. But she knew that her father struggled every day to see it fresh.

"But Dad, I've got…"

"No, just a minute Rosie," said her father, gazing at the image. "Look how it was, so astonishingly bold and sophisticated." Rosie knew that word; it was what they'd said she'd looked when she'd tried on her first pair of reading glasses. Although she often didn't understand all the words her father used, she almost always knew what he meant. Now his fingertip traced the central curving line which ran from the tip of the Horse's tail to the top of its left ear.

"See, Rosie, see how much you can leave out of a picture, and how that doesn't lessen, but can actually increase, the impression you want to convey. The curve of that sickle-shaped rear right leg – how the bulge at its top suggests the big thigh muscles, without being weighed down by actually having to draw them. And see how the completely separate boomerang of the rear left leg suggests bunched, hoof-flying movement!

"And the subtlety of that wish-bone fork at the top of the right fore-leg, the necessary connection with the neck and torso, depicted in just two thin lines, and one of them uncompleted. And then the spindly near-side fore-leg, which your mother says is what a horse leads with at the gallop – it's so masterly, racing out just beyond of the thrust-forward head."

But then he sighed. "The head! A bird's head! But what kind of bird, and why? And who did it? And if it was a banner, why can you hardly ever see it whole? I'm still no nearer to…"

"Dad!" cried Rosie, who could contain herself no longer. "Dad, listen! I've found an old BSA!"

The effect on her father was instant, and electrifying. He jumped to his feet, nearly knocking his chair over, peered at Rosie intently, and said

"A BSA! Where?"

Looking back later, Rosie thought that one of the better parts she had played in the whole story had been guessing that her Dad might be interested in the motorbike at all. He rarely spoke of

28

his days as a student when he used to ride one, and had never talked about getting another. But now he was absolutely galvanized, breaking off work, which he never did, to walk quickly across the fields to the barn and look for himself.

Rosie's mother Mary, busy cooking lunch, was astonished to see him flying out, and called Rosie back as she went to go with him. Mary Ransom was a handsome blond lady with long straight hair and a wide mouth, who had often been compared to a TV presenter called Anneka Rice with a show called 'Challenge Anneka'. Mrs Honeywell had had a word with Mary, so that she knew what had happened, but she seemed as surprised as Rosie by her husband the Professor's burst of enthusiasm.

"Rose, you've worked a miracle," she laughed, "you've got Daddy out of his study before dark! Now come and give me a hand with this cake," she said.

"But Mum, I want to go with him!" cried Rosie

"No, you've done enough walking for now," said her Mum gently but firmly. "And Mrs Wilsden couldn't come today, so I really could do with some help." In fact she had another, unspoken reason for wanting to keep Rosie near.

Mrs Honeywell had said that they were welcome to keep the old bike, and had even left the papers, documents and the photo, in case they did want it. The farm lady would accept no money, and when Mary had pressed her, had just told the Professor's wife that she could help with the cream teas at the farm again, if she wanted to do anything. But she had also said that her father's accident with the tractor had happened long ago, in 1958, and both women had guessed that the motorbike might be too rotted and rusting to be worth putting right again. Now Mary didn't know which of them would be more disappointed if that did prove to be the case, her husband or her daughter. She was glad to see that Rosie was soon absorbed, mixing the flour and measuring out the currants and glace cherries, not to mention sampling a few for herself.

But this lull did not last long. Within an hour Rosie's father burst in again, overflowing with excitement.

"It's remarkable!" he cried. "Absolutely complete and original. A BSA A10 650 twin, just like the one I had when I was a student! These time capsule bikes, historic machines that haven't been mucked about, they're getting rarer and rarer," he went on to his wife. "Well done, Rosie! And you too, Zoe, of course," he added, rubbing the dog's head, as the black labrador had caught the mood of excitement and was running around them in circles, lashing her tail against the red Aga.

"But dear…" said Rosie's Mum in a worried voice, for now that the old bike had passed from being a possible disappointment to a matter of vital interest, Mary Ransom had another worry.

Despite her husband's job with the well-known Archaeological Team at Oxford nearby, the family was not well off. Years before when the Team under Professor Ransom had first investigated the White Horse, there had been plenty of money from sponsors to fund the work. The results had been interesting but not earth-shattering, and the Team had moved on to other things, both around Oxford, and in places as different as the Tower of London and the Channel Tunnel.

But Roderick Ransom, perhaps because he had grown up in the Vale, had remained locked into his obsession with the Horse, often working on it at his own expense. The family still had his salary, but the Team as a whole had suffered from his lack of interest in the new projects, and recently funding had got very thin indeed. Rosie's mother knew that there was now the real possibility that the Team would have to close down and that her husband would lose his job, unless the Professor or someone else on the unit produced some spectacular results, to grab the headlines and attract the big sponsors' funds.

So this was not really the time to be getting involved in the time-consuming and probably expensive business of restoring an old motorbike. But looking at her husband's face, suddenly boyish again after long months of grinding, fruitless struggle at work, Mary

Ransom hadn't the heart to mention it.

The Professor however, oblivious to all that, hurried on, "And Lorna Honeywell says we can have it! In fact I popped up there and had a word, and her boy Tom's bringing it down on a trailer after lunch! Now, what's that delicious smell? Let's eat!"

That afternoon Tom Honeywell and his uncle pulled slowly into the drive of the Ransom's cottage, with the BSA strapped down to a trailer behind the dark green Land Rover. But when the men and Rosie's Dad had manhandled it down from the trailer, and parked it in front of the garden shed which her Dad had cleared out for the bike to live in, even Rosie felt her heart sink. The motorbike was a mess.

In the daylight she could see now that it wasn't just a matter of the splintered headlamp glass and flat tyres. The BSA looked truly shabby. Cobwebs connected every surface, and all its paint and chrome were flaking away from the grimy metal and red rust. The same falling beam that had smashed the lamp had put a big ugly dent in the petrol tank, which at that point had rotted away. And all the metal of the engine was covered in nasty white furry stuff. The chain at the back drooped, the corroded tubular silencers tilted up at crazy angles on their own, where the exhausts pipes that led to them from the engine had simply rotted away. The seat's cover was full of holes and the rotting, nibbled foam within exposed where, she guessed, those mice had used it for their nests. When Rosie reached out for the handlebar grips, they crumbled, leaving black goo on her hands. The BSA really was a mess. It was hard to imagine that it would ever go again.

Her father, however, was undismayed. He pointed out to Tom little touches like the original metal badges on the tank, and the tiny tin shield still fastened to the rear of the seat, bearing the name of the Northampton dealers that had first sold the bike. While they were busy with all that, Rosie went quietly to the front of the Land Rover, where her sharp eyes had spotted the old riding coat – and the helmet. She reached inside, picked up the bowl-shaped crash helmet, and pulled it onto her head again.

"'Allow Rosie," said the familiar voice faintly. "Boompy ride down here! But that young Land Rowver was interesting. They're from Brumijum too, yunow, made in Solihull. Only he didn't now nothing when I asked him about the BSA."

The men were looking at Rosie and laughing at the sight of her with the helmet on her head, so she couldn't say 'Which BSA?' But she'd thought it, and the voice replied

"The *BSA*. That's what we call the place at Small 'Eath in Brumijum, where they mek us. A ginormous place it is, but that young Land Rowver niver heard of it…"

So the bike could read her thoughts! But at that point Rosie had to snatch off the helmet, as her mother was bearing down on her with a horrified expression, which Rosie guessed had to do with the cobwebs and dust covering the helmet, inside and out. So she stepped towards her father and said quickly

"Dad, please may I keep the old helmet? *Please?* I'll clean it out."

"You want the pudding-basin crash hat, do you?" laughed the Professor. He took it from her hands and looked inside. "And this was a good one – an Everoak TT. A bit past its sell-by now, but if you clean it up, yes, you can keep it to play with. For finding the bike," he added hastily, as his wife gave him a look which Rosie guessed meant that Mum wasn't very pleased, and that her Dad hadn't heard the last of it. Rosie clutched the helmet to her, while the Professor turned back to study the BSA.

"She's in quite a state," he said, shaking his head. "We'd better call in an expert," and when his wife gave him a questioning look, explained:

"Mike the Bike."

The next day, which was Sunday, Mike the Bike roared into the drive on his own motorbike, which he called 'The Humph'.

"*Hu*sqvarna frame with a Tri*umph* engine," he explained to Rosie. " Hu-umph, see?" Rosie had never heard of the Husk-thingy, and the roaring Triumph engine didn't look or sound 'lady-like' to her, but she smiled and kept quiet. If Mike would help them, there was a much better chance of getting the BSA to run again.

Mike, a short figure, climbed off the Humph and limped over to the shed to look at the rusty bike. Her Dad had told Rosie that Mike had been a paratrooper in the Army, and had been wounded in a war. With his thick glasses, long greasy hair and perpetual grin, he didn't look like Rosie's idea of a soldier.

Now he ran a small shop in a nearby town, repairing and selling old motorbikes, new scooters, and bicycles. Rosie and her Dad had gone there to buy her first proper bicycle, a handsome purple Raleigh, which Mike had sold them second-hand. Mike and his family lived over the shop, and while they had been there, Mike's young son had showed Rosie his chipmunk, which some of the time ranged free in his bedroom, quick as a bird and performing amazing leaps and climbs. Her Dad talked to Mike about the new 'old' motorbikes the shop sold, which were nearly the same as the real old ones, and came from India. They dropped in when possible to chat and buy things for her bicycle, particularly after a snake had joined the chipmunk, and Rosie could watch it being fed its dinner of dead mice from the freezer. And now Mike's hour had come.

"A proper barn find, eh, Rosie? You done good," said Mike in his London accent, as he limped round the BSA, his eyes moving as ceaselessly as his son's chipmunk. He bent to put his hand on the pedal sticking out of the bike's right hand side, the kick-starter, and strained downwards, but couldn't move it. "It's not what's on the outside that counts," he went on quietly, "it's what's inside," as he felt around underneath the engine.

Then Rosie's Mum and Dad came out from the house, the Professor carrying the bag of papers for the bike, which Mrs Honeywell had found. It was another sunny April morning, and soon they all sat down with drinks at the garden table by the back door, coffee for the grown-ups, milk for Rosie.

"Well Ace," said Mike to Rosie's Dad, "which d'you want first, the good news or the bad news?"

"Oh, let's have the bad news," said her Dad in mock gloom, his eyes sparkling with interest.

"Well it's genuinely dead original like you said," Mike began. "But it's also dead knackered. Where d'you want me to start? Tyres and inner tubes shot, all the electrics, wheels that need rebuilding, a seized-up swinging-arm at the back – at the front the forks could be mostly OK but they'll be rotten from the seals up, so you'll need new stanchions. And that's not even mentioning the engine. Now if we're very lucky there, all the engine oil will have dropped down to the bottom and protected it – so the bottom end, the crankshaft and big ends, *could* be in good nick. The gearbox will probably be OK. But the top end is solid – the pistons have probably seized to the bores…"

Maybe it was the word "bore", but at this point Rosie couldn't stop herself asking

"What are pistons?"

"They're things like an upside-down metal mug with no

handle," said her father. "They go up and down extremely fast in round holes, the cylinder bores, which have been, well, bored out in the metal cylinder block. That whizzing up-and-down is basically what makes the motorbike go, like you pedalling your bicycle. On our BSA there are two of these cylinders, which is why we call it a 'twin', for twin cylinders – some motorbikes have just one, they're 'singles'.

"And that'll learn you, Rosie," laughed Mike, "see what happens when you start asking questions. No, couldn't have put it better myself, Professor. And if we're really lucky again, soaking in light oil and then a good clout with a mallet will free up the pistons and rings. But it's odds on the bores will be rusty. If so, we're talking a re-bore, with new rings and pistons…"

"Goodness," said Rosie's mother nervously, "it all sounds as if it might be terribly expensive…"

"A re-bore and plus 20 pistons?" said Mike, who was looking through the bike's documents with what Rosie noticed immediately was sharply increasing interest. "Probably about a hundred and twenty quid. But I read somewhere that there's a bit over three thousand parts on an old British twin, and an awful lot of them are going to need replacing on this one. The Professor's told me he's handy with the spanners, which will save you a bit of money. But even doing some of the work yourself, you're probably looking at a bill for a bit more than two thousand pounds."

Mike's last words hung in the air between the four of them. Rosie grabbed her father's hand as Mike went on, "Which is roughly what the bike will be worth when you're finished. But that doesn't take into account all your time and trouble. So the question you have to ask yourself, is: do I really want to do this?"

"Yes," said Professor Ransom without hesitating, as Rosie squeezed his hand. "I do, but…"

"No," said Mike, holding up his palm, "that's all I wanted to hear. Because I haven't got to the good news yet, see? First of all, in the back of my workshop I've got a BSA, a '57 B31 single with a blown-up engine. And as you'll no doubt know, Professor, BSA twins and singles at that time shared most of their running gear – except for the engines, they were pretty well the same! So there's a petrol tank in fair order to replace your one with the hole, and a decent seat, and probably a carburettor, and a lot of other things, all of which I'll let you have for a bit less than an arm and a leg…"

"But two thousand pounds…" murmured Mary.

" 'Ang about, darling," said Mike, "I told you there was good news as well. And I mean *really* good news." He held up the green concertina of cardboard, the BSA's old log book, in one hand, and the V5 registration paper in the other. "With these, you know what you can do?"

As one, three Ransom heads shook 'No'.

"If you'd only had this," said Mike holding up the green card, "you could have still claimed the number plate back. Otherwise, because the number wasn't in circulation in the 1970s when the registration numbers went computerised, that number would have been lost. But with evidence like this," grinned Mike, waving the green concertina, "you could definitely have claimed it back. But after that, you'd have had to keep it on the vehicle."

"Well that's very nice," said Rosie's Mum weakly, "but I don't see how…"

"But with *this*," Mike went on, holding up the V5, "you've got the number already. And – you can sell it."

"Hold on," said her father excitedly, "that's right, isn't it? When they started putting extra letters before or after registrations, the ones that were just three letters and two or three numbers began to be worth money. You see lists of them in the back of the newspapers. People, numbers dealers, have made fortunes…"

"I do a bit of that," said Mike. "Any three letter/three figure number is worth at least £400," he went on. "But special ones, like 'L-U-V', or 'B-S-A', they're worth more. A lot more. And when it's someone's name…"

Rosie cried "A-N-N! That's 'Ann'!"

"Bingo," said Mike. "And *that's* worth anything between four and six thousand pounds! But," he held up his hand, "there's something else as well as just the letters. Don't let's forget the numbers…"

"What were they?" said the Professor.

"9-1-1," said Rosie, puzzled.

"Nine eleven! Like the Porsche 911 sports car!" yelled her Dad.

"Professor, go to the top of the class," laughed Mike the Bike.

"But…" said Rosie, "but if you sell her number plate, she'll lose her name! 'Ann', that's what I was going to call her."

"Don't worry, darling," said Mike reassuringly. "I've got a better one, and it's not too far from 'Ann', neither. We'll call her Anneka – cos she's going to be a bit of a challenge!"

R osie could not believe that anyone would really be silly enough to pay thousands of pounds for a number plate for their wife's sports car, but it soon proved to be true.

Within a week Mike had, as he put it, 'done the business', and one morning in the post, there was a letter from him with a very large cheque indeed. Her parents went rather quiet when they saw exactly how large the sum was, and they never told Rosie how much, which made her quite cross. But she understood that there was going to be plenty to do up the bike, and a good bit over besides.

However, to start with it looked as if the money, however much it was, would not be coming to them, and so would not help get the BSA going again. Her father insisted, and her mother agreed, that they should offer it all to Mrs Honeywell, the bike's rightful owner, straight away.

But the farm lady wouldn't hear of it. "Finder's keepers," she said. "Your girl Rosie found the bike, and the Professor will do it up, so it's only fair. And that's what would have made my Dad Wilf happy, so that's the way we'll do it." It took a long, long visit to the farm, a three-bottle lamb feed for Rosie, before her father could persuade Mrs Honeywell at least to accept half the money. Once she had agreed, she admitted that after the recent foot-and-mouth trouble, and with the way farming was now, the money would be very welcome. "But," she concluded, "I want first go on the pillion when you've done the bike – after Rosie, of course," she added hastily. "So I can see if I like it any better than I did the last time!"

Meanwhile Rosie was back at the village school, in the shadow of the tall old church with its octagonal tower, which they called 'the Cathedral of the Vale'. The weather was staying fine, so morning breaks saw the children out in the playground. Which was its usual noisy, complicated self.

Rosie was having a word with her particular friend Ernest. Ernest was lively but slightly built, looked like an elf, and lived up to his name by talking slowly and deliberately at all times. People were always saying he was Rosie's boyfriend, which was silly, as both of them knew very well that they were really just friends.

But that did not stop Bill Grant, a fleshy, lumbering boy two years older than Rosie, from a large, rough village family, swaggering up to them and chanting "Boyfriend! Boyfriend!" at Rosie. Ernest said nothing, because unfortunately he wanted nothing more than to be Bill Grant's best friend – the playground really *was* complicated – while Rosie said nothing because she was a bit scared. In the face of her silence, Bill stuck his clenched fist under Rosie's nose and said

"Know what that smells of?" And when she shook her head, Bill roared " 'Orspital!" before lumbering off to threaten one of his younger brothers. Rosie asked Ernest if he'd like to come and see the BSA after school, before running off to join her friend Anna and the other girls at their safe spot over by the wheelie bins. But before she could get there, the bell rang.

In the tall classroom, shafts of sunlight caught dust motes floating lazily in the warm air, and it was hard to concentrate on what Miss Haycraft was saying about Modern Art, even though it was quite interesting. Apparently this painter – something like 'Pickandmix-o' – or was it 'Capisco'? – had painted pictures so that if you looked at the faces in them one way, it was like seeing them from ahead, but then if you looked at it another way, it was like seeing them from the side. Rosie doodled a nose with an eye in it, but her mind slid off to the thought of the three thousand pieces in the BSA, and how they were ever going to get them all clean.

Luckily it was not too long until lunch, where she sat next to Anna, and the pudding was chocolate sponge covered in chocolate custard sprinkled with chocolate hundreds-and-thousands. This made Rosie remember a time once on holiday in France, when a grave young waitress in a restaurant by a river, when her Dad had asked what the French word for them was, had told them that in the kitchen the chocolate sprinkles were called '*crottes de souris*', and her Dad had eventually explained that this meant mouse poo. Rosie told Anna, and they giggled so hard that they almost couldn't finish their pudding.

Rosie lived about a mile outside the village, so if she wanted someone to come and play with her, her Mum had to check with their Mum that it was OK, and then drive them out to the cottage, and afterwards drive them home again. Sometimes it wasn't convenient, and Rosie would be left feeling lonely. But today Ernest's Mum said it would be fine if he came to tea, and soon they were jumping out of the car, running across the gravel drive, climbing the five-bar gate and sprinting into the garden, with Zoe delirious to have Rosie home as well as someone new to play with.

Rosie ran to the wooden playhouse her mother had built for her third birthday, to fetch out her purple bicycle. But when she came out with the pushbike, she stopped in horror.

Her Dad had left the door of the shed with the BSA in it open, and Ernest had gone straight inside. Now he had come out again – and half of his elfin face was obscured by the pudding-basin helmet, which he had picked up from the saddle and jammed onto his head.

Rosie held her breath, but Ernest's expression was just its usual serious-looking frown. Cautiously she called out

"Can you…can you hear anything?"

Ernest's frown deepened. He lifted the helmet's leather

flaps clear of his ears and said loudly

"I can hear you. Now."

"But can you hear – anything else?" said Rosie carefully. For though she liked Ernest very much, and as a rule was not very good at keeping secrets, something had told her that this talking business should really be kept between herself and Anneka the BSA. She felt that very strongly.

Suddenly Ernest's expression changed.

"Yes," he said slowly, "I can, I can hear something." He paused. "I can hear your Mum calling us for tea…"

As he pulled off the helmet and went in, Rosie took it from him and put it on. A familiar voice said in her ear

"Daon't wurry, Rosie. Oi daon't talk to just anyone, y'know!"

L ater on Rosie would think that, though the process of getting Anneka going again taught her a lot of different things, the one big thing that she learned from it, was patience.

The business had started out briskly enough. Even before the money had been sorted out, her father had bought a can of special oil, and after spraying it several times on the nuts which fastened the bits where the wheels turned, and waiting for a couple of days, he was able to undo them, take the wheels off the BSA, and turn them over to Mike the Bike for rebuilding. Anneka had to be propped up on bricks and logs from the woodpile so she wouldn't fall over.

Meanwhile Mike had come to take the big electrical bits. "This tube in front of the engine is the dynamo, for the lights and so on," Mike had explained to Rosie. "And this one behind the engine is the important one – the magneto" (he said it 'mag-neat-oh'). "For the ignition – the sparks. What makes Anneka's pistons go up and down is a big bang when the petrol-gas explodes, and what makes *that* happen is a spark, at just the right time. And it comes from the magneto."

"Is that why they call these 'sparking plugs'?" said Rosie, holding up one of the chunky little threaded plugs which her Dad had coaxed out of the top of the engine, before pouring more oil down the holes that they lived in.

"Spot on," said Mike.

"But why does there have to be so much *oil?*" Rosie complained, using an old rag to wipe her hands, which were now oily just from holding the sparking plug.

"Oil and grease are what makes the wheels go round," said Mike. "The spindle in the wheel hub, the pistons in the bores, they're all metal, and rubbing up against each other really fast. Pretty soon they get hot – I mean *really* hot, hot enough to melt together and do what we call 'seize', lock up solid. Oil is what stops them, what makes the metal bits where they touch slippery, and cool. Oil makes it all happen."

He took the electrical bits off to his expert to have them rebuilt. At the same time her father had sprayed the special oil on the nuts and bolts which fastened the engine onto the tubes of the frame. Rosie came back from school one day to find a gaping hole where Anneka's engine had been. Mike had come round again and helped her Dad lift it out of the frame, and now the engine sat on the sturdy workbench in the shed, ready for the Professor to take it apart.

And that was when Rosie really began to learn patience. It wasn't just the soaking with oil and waiting. Some of the nuts and screws simply wouldn't turn. Her father was surprisingly calm, but sometimes things snapped off, and there was more difficult work getting what was left out. Sometimes they had to get Mike to heat up the nuts which had stuck with a little blowtorch, till they glowed cherry red. Rosie would squeeze her eyes tight shut, frightened that it might be torture for Anneka, but the calm voice in her ears told her not to fret. Rosie tried to make the bike feel better by constantly decking the rusty handlebars with daisy chains and garlands of the pretty purple weed-flowers from the garden. Anneka seemed to like this.

They got the side-covers on the bottom of the engine off, with more oily sludge gushing out as they did so. Her father was delighted, and showed Rosie how all the metal bits inside, once the oil had been wiped off, were as good as new even after forty years or more. As they had hoped, the oil had seen to that. There was just a tiny bit of rust on top of the chain which lived in there, as the oil hadn't been able to cover that far up. Rosie began to see the point of oil.

She liked helping in the shed. There were always bits to wipe clean and polish. Sometimes some of that work was boring and made her fingers hurt. But then there were bits she enjoyed, like taking the oil tank which had been sludgy inside, filling it with old nuts and bolts and some paraffin, and then shaking it about noisily, on and on, to loosen off the muck within it. It was like playing the maracas at school, only louder.

Her father also gave her the workshop manual book for BSA twins, and it was her job to read out the instructions. And when she was doing this, she would casually put on the helmet, so Anneka could give her a running commentary. Once, for instance, when the Professor was working on the frame and trying to unbolt a footrest, the voice in her ear had called

" 'Ere, ar kid – 'e's doing it the wrong way! 'E's toightening me bolt up, not loosening it off…"

"Dad," said Rosie, hesitantly, for the veins were standing out on her father's forehead, "are you sure you're going the right way with that?"

"Why," panted her father, "does the book say clockwise?"

"I think so," said Rosie. Her father applied his strength on the spanner in the opposite direction, and nearly toppled forward as the nut suddenly gave. It would not be the last time that Anneka helped with her own strip-down and rebuild.

An exciting moment came when they took off the ruined petrol tank and found, on its underside, an unfaded, unrusted area of the bright red paint. The Professor chipped off a flake of it, and popped it in a clear plastic bag to deliver to Mike, so that his paint expert could make up an exact match for Anneka's new tank.

When her father had gone in one day, Rosie, still with the helmet on, sat looking at the old dark orange tin tray, which her mother had given them to help keep odd bits together. The tray had a picture on it of a cross-looking Japanese bird, something like

a heron, standing on one leg in some reeds and looking beady. All over the big tray were nuts, bolts, old wires, springs and cables, the red plastic tail light, the kick-start lever, parts without number.

Then she asked Anneka a question that had been puzzling her.

"Now you're in bits," Rosie said, "which part of you is talking to me? I mean, which bit of you is the *real* you?"

Anneka thought for a while.

"Dunno," replied the faint voice which the bike had had since the strip-down had begun. "What oi felt was, oi came alive, really alive, running down the road. The faster the better! But oi haven't done that in a long while, and oi'm still talking to you…Oi mean, do people have a bit that's the real them? That stays the same if they lose a bit o' themselves, or they change from being kids to grown-oops?"

"I don't know," said Rosie softly, looking out of the shed door at the garden in the evening. "I think so." Because, perhaps surprisingly for a young girl, she did think quite a lot about that question.

There was another thing on her mind about Anneka, while the white cow parsley which Rosie loved began to froth beside the lanes, as May edged towards June.

As well as the workshop manual, when her father had seen that Rosie was genuinely interested in the motorbike, he lent her one of his books, with pictures of bikes and a short history of the BSA Company in it. Rosie then discovered that after the factory at Small Heath in Birmingham had survived the German bombing early in the Second World War, it had produced a lot of the guns, as well as a lot of Army motorbikes, which had helped the British win that war – after all, the company's sign, echoed in the faded, peeling transfers on Anneka's sides, had been three rifles propped up against each other.

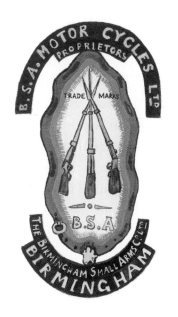

Rosie found that for some time, one out of every four motorbikes had been a BSA, including little red ones for the Post Office, and big yellow motorcycles and sidecars, like Wallace and Grommit's, for the AA men who helped you when your car broke down. But in the end, big as BSA had been, the company had come to grief, and a few years after that, the great factory at Small Heath, where thousands of men and women had worked all their lives, had been knocked down and built over. And that was ages ago, more than twenty years before Rosie had been born!

How was she going to tell Anneka?

The opportunity arose after they had been waiting over two weeks for new top bits for the front forks. The rest of the forks had been OK, but her father said that, as Mike had guessed, from the seals upwards he had found that they were rotten, and Mike had sent off for the new bits. But they hadn't come.

"If 'e needs new stanchions," Anneka snorted one evening when Rosie was alone with her, "why don't 'e shoot up to Brum and pick up a pair from the BSA? It's not that far."

"Anneka," said Rosie, "Dad lent me a book about BSA, and I've…"

" 'Ere, did it tell yow about the War?" asked the bike eagerly. " At Small 'Eath oi was once parked next to an Army bike in for reconditioning, and it'd been being built the noight of the Big Blitz. The enemy planes could find the BSA easy, cos we 'ad our own railway track and canal, and they'd just follow them to the works. It were a broight moonlit noight, and they dropped incendiaries an' mines and oil bombs, and brought the New Building and all the machines in it down on the men and women sheltering on the ground floor there. When the All Clear sounded, eighty-one people had died, and a lorra machine tools were destroyed, but after that they worked harder than ever and helped win the War…"

"Anneka, I know," Rosie broke in. "But it's all gone now. The factory. Everything."

"Gerroff!" said the old bike, but its voice was full of fear. After a while there came a mutter of "Fuddeffinit? But that place was magic! You'd see men and women come in and get hit by the smell of new paint, new rubber an' fresh oil, and just stand there, all a-tingle! It was loike a big family; in fact a lot of them *were* brothers and sisters, fathers and sons. And proud of the work, aye. All that? All gone?"

"I'm afraid so," said Rosie. "They pulled the factory down over twenty-five years ago." All she could think of to say next was, "Did you ever see the White Horse?"

"Yeh," said the voice dully, "the old gaffer, the farmer, would roide by there most days. But oi can't think o' that now. Oi've gorra pine. What's the point of getting going again. All gone…"

"What I mean," said Rosie, "is that my Dad says there used to be a great fort up above the Horse, with houses and hundreds of soldiers and people and animals. And that's all gone now, the buildings and all the people.

"But the Horse is still there." She paused. "You could be like the Horse. When they see you and hear you and watch you run, people could still know how things used to be?"

There was a long silence. Then the voice came, growling quietly.

"Yer right, ar kid. We'll show 'em what we could mek, when we put our mind to it!"

Next morning, another fine one, Rosie drove with her father to Mike the Bike's shop. They took the unfaded paint chip, for Mike's paint expert to use as a match when he mixed up the correct shade of red. The Professor would then spray this on the petrol tank, the one off the other BSA which Mike had told them about. They also took the engine's iron barrels for reboring. Things were coming on.

At the shop, Rosie went to look at Mike's son's chipmunk, but after a while the boy had to retrieve the amazingly agile creature from halfway up the curtains, put it back in its cage and go out to meet his friends. As Rosie came downstairs, she bumped into her father going out to the car with an arm-full of shiny metal bits and pieces.

"Look at this, Rose," he said enthusiastically. "Here's the seat off that other BSA." He held up a ridged saddle, curved like a black caterpillar. "It's not standard, but I sat on it, and it was very comfortable. And here's the petrol tank – see how good the chrome is! And the oil tank and mudguards – they've been chromed too – Anneka's going to be a very smart girl indeed! Especially after I fix that winged lady figure, which I kept from my old bike, onto her front mudguard. Listen, I've got a couple of quick things to do in town. Why don't you watch Mike at work for a bit?"

Rosie didn't really want to, but before she could argue,

her father had bustled off. So she went out of the shop's back door, and crossing a small back yard littered with old motorbikes in various states of repair, entered the workshop.

The place was like a cave, with a slanted metal roof above, set with corrugated plastic panels to let some light in. On a warm day like this one, it became very hot. Every inch of the walls and most of the floor were covered with bits of bikes, hanging on wires or stacked on racks, along with containers of nuts, bolts, cables, springs and what seemed to be most of the three thousand parts you needed to build a motorcycle.

When Mike had a blowtorch going or was hammering something straight, the shadowy place seemed like the blacksmith's forge which Rosie had visited. And it was funny; her father had once said that all the smiths in the old stories had limped, like Mike did. In fact Mike's other name was Smith, and more than once Rosie had wondered idly if he was descended from Wayland Smith, the blacksmith to the old gods. He was supposed to have lived along the Ridgeway about a mile from the White Horse, at Waylands Smithy.

This was a beautiful circle of tall trees, with grave caves in the centre of it. The story was that if you left your horse and a piece of money there overnight, in the morning your animal would have new horseshoes. But Rosie would never leave a pony of hers up there at night, as even in the twilight, the place could be rather spooky. Her father had told her that when he had been a boy, no birds had ever sung in those wonderful trees.

But Rosie had heard plenty of birds during the times she and her father used to go there when she'd been little. Her father liked to tell people the story of how one afternoon, when Rosie had been three, she had been out of sight exploring in the grave caves. A serious man and woman had arrived to view the place, and had got a big shock when Rosie's head had popped out of the grave entrance and enquired cheerfully, "Cuppa tea?"

"Not a bad greeting for them from the Otherworld," her father would laugh.

Now Mike the Bike, wearing a grimy brown shopman's coat, looked up from his work, peering at her over the top of his thick glasses, and said cheerfully " 'Allo Rosie, come to see how Anneka's getting along? If only she could talk and tell us herself, eh?" Luckily he didn't notice Rosie's flushed face as he rattled on, "You're just in time – I'm going to bead-blast her outer engine covers."

"Bead-blast?" said Rosie.

"Yeah, watch this," said Mike, flicking on a noisy extractor fan, and picking up one of the curved metal covers in his gloved left hand. He pushed hand and cover through a shrouded hole into a large glass-fronted cabinet marked "Vacu-Blast International". Then his right hand also went in there, to grasp a pistol-like thing with a nozzle.

When he hit the trigger, a vapour-like spray of what Mike said were tiny polythene pellets was fired at the tarnished metal cover. " It's OK, it won't try and blast the piece out of my hand," laughed Mike. Rosie watched mesmerised as slowly, slowly, where the stream of spray bombarded it, one end of the cover in a creeping line went silvery bright. The extractor was humming noisily without let-up. "If you don't put it on," said Mike loudly as he took a moment's break, "stuff blows out of the top and you get covered in grit. Oops, look, I missed a bit," and switching the gun back on again, bent to his work. And it was work, with Mike intent over the piece for twenty minutes or more.

When he finally pulled out the cleaned up cover, it emerged with a matt silver finish, and Mike slipped it straight into a large clear plastic bag. "We could have polished it," he told Rosie, "but that takes a lot longer, and Anneka's going to be for riding, not showing. So just blasting is fine. Tell your Dad if he gets fingerprints on the cover when he fits it back on, to wash them off with petrol, nothing else. And then to wash his hands! This petrol today is nasty stuff."

Mike set the bag down by the door, his face glistening with sweat. "Warm now," he said, and slipped off his brown coat.

Rosie stood motionless at what she saw.

Mike was wearing an old black tee shirt with the sleeves cut off, and she could now see that every inch of his muscular arms was covered in tattoos. And they were the same swirling, intricate designs which she had seen so often in the pictures on the walls of her father's office.

Mike saw her gazing, and laughed a little awkwardly. "Me Celtic warrior tattoos. From when I was still in the Mob – you know, the Army."

"Why were you a soldier?" asked Rose without thinking. "My Mum says fighting is wrong."

"And she's probably right and all," said Mike. His glasses were reflecting the light, so that Rosie couldn't see his eyes. "I was just younger then, and full of daft ideas. But I'll tell you one thing. It may be wrong, but when you're in the Army and especially when you're fighting, there's nothing like the feeling you have for your pals. I love Janet and the children, but I'm sorry, it's a different thing to what I felt for my mates down in the South Atlantic, when the bombs and bullets started to fly. And it was weird – when we were all together, the more them bombs and bullets came to snuff us, the more we seemed to feel alive. Only now I can see, that feeling, and the one we had between us, absolutely couldn't last. I mean, how *could* it last, when what made it happen was us putting our lives on the line together, night and day.

"Well, that all ended for me when I stepped in the wrong place," said Mike, tapping his bad leg. "And I was one of the lucky ones, in a way. Not all my friends came home. But I'll bet it was the same for those Celtic warriors, when it was chariots, axes and spears, up on the Horse. You very quickly forget what started it, why you're fighting. You only care about your brothers in arms…"

Then Mike shook himself. "Sorry, Rosie, I don't know what come over me. You don't want to hear about that stuff – my boys start groaning now if I even mention the Mob. Listen, here's another little job for us – spoking up. Or knitting wheels, as I call it." Mike limped over to the workbench and began unwrapping spirals of greased brown paper from the gleaming circle of a chromed wheel rim. When that was done, he reached under the bench and produced one of Anneka's bare wheel centres, with the old spokes all cut off it. He sat this on the bench in the middle of the shiny circle of the rim.

Next he unwrapped a bundle of new spokes, which were hooked over at one end and threaded at the other. Rosie couldn't believe that these spindly pieces of thin metal would take the whole weight of a big bike. But Mike showed her how each spoke had an opposite number on the other side of the central hub, so that loads were shared, and when you put the brakes on, for instance, the forces were absorbed.

Soon they were lost in the intricacies of the spokes' pattern. " You've got 'overs' and 'unders'," said Mike. It was really tricky, the outermost spokes had to be made to cross the two beneath them, while on the rim, the dimpled spoke holes looked the same but were pointing in different directions. It needed careful thought, and even the experienced Mike ended up having to undo some spokes on one side after he had taken them by mistake in the same direction as the ones on the other side. When it was time to screw all the spokes down, Rosie was allowed to do a few, but it was difficult.

The loose spokes let the hub shift about, and under her hands the wheel felt like a live thing.

When Professor Ransom finally appeared in the workshop doorway, they were still at it. Rosie felt very pleased when Mike told her father that she'd "done good". Mike turned to the other, finished wheel, which was sitting up in what he called a jig, two upright metal legs bolted to the bench with the wheel suspended between them. He spun the wheel and ran a screwdriver along the spokes, which gave back a musical metallic "Drr-rr-ing."

"Spokesong," said Mike, "tells you it's right, all the spokes equally tensioned. If you hear sort of a dull, lifeless clunk, you've got a loose one. I'll drop the wheels round when I'm done, Prof. We have to skim the hubs, and put in new brake linings, where that white corrosion got under the linings and lifted them off the shoes."

The work rebuilding Anneka sometimes seemed never-ending, but at least Rosie felt they had seen some progress that morning. While her Dad picked up the clean engine covers in their plastic sacks, Rosie wandered out of the shadowy workshop into the brilliant sunlight, feeling that she was stepping out from another world.

Rosie and her father drove back from Mike's shop along the winding, up-and-down road following the base of the Downs. The creamy cow parsley frothed in the hedges like the foaming top on a fizzy drink that you've poured too fast, and along the avenue before the turn to their village, the tall beech trees had unfurled their beautiful, tremulous green leaves. As they drove along with the windows down, the spare parts for Anneka clanked gently in the back of the car.

But when they reached the crossroads where they would normally turn down to their village, without a word spoken the Professor kept driving onwards, into the sunlight, and Rosie knew exactly why, and smiled to herself. They drove along the tortuous bit of road where she and the dog had walked that first morning, up and down past the bushes decked with Old Man's Beard. They passed the field with the caravan and the entrance to Mrs Honeywell's farm, and finally turned left at the next crossroads, onto the narrow, winding track that snaked its way up White Horse Hill.

With a great jangle from the metal in the back, they crossed the cattle grid beneath the Roman Camp, the steep round bump of a hill on their right, which faced the slope that carried the Horse itself. Then they were climbing the flank of the Hill, rising higher and swinging to the right up along the Hill's shoulder, as the whole grandness of the Vale, and of the wavy slopes above the valley of the Manger, came into their view. Rosie's spirits lifted, as they always did, and she knew that her father felt the same.

Up and up they climbed, and at the top parked for a moment where they shouldn't have, in the little space kept for disabled drivers, facing out to overlook the Vale. They got out of the car, and stood in the sunshine. Rosie felt the wind whipping her long fair hair. The green Vale stretched away in front of them into the hazy distance, punctuated by the unmistakable outline of the tower called Faringdon Folly on its wooded hilltop. Rosie watched a crow flying steadily against the wind across the land below them, until her eyes were arrested by the long pale line of a train moving in the opposite direction.

"When I was a boy," said her Dad, "it was easier to see the trains. Because of the steam," he explained.

Out of sight down to their left lay the proper car park, cleverly concealed in what had once been a quarry, where the flaky white stone had been dug that was built into their cottage. A thin line of visitors, with dogs on leads and children, was trekking slowly up across the slopes towards them, like pilgrims in ancient times; but in the ever-present wind from the west, these pilgrims were often flying kites.

That was how Rosie thought of White Horse Hill – great days kite-flying, with the reel of string clipped to her belt so that it wouldn't be whipped from hands and the kite lost, with her mother helping her, as her father told her how the wind would have quickly shredded banners in the old days, which might explain why they had carved the Horse on the hill, as a sort of permanent banner. And doing roly-polys with her Dad down the steep slopes of the hill fort, earth-sky-earth-sky-earth-sky as they lay face to face bumping and tumbling over and over down the hill, shrieking and giggling helplessly as her father shook with laughter while he kept her safe with his braced elbows. And walks, great walks, from the times when she had been carried up the Hill on her parents' backs in a rucksack, to the days when she was under her own steam, stumbling after Zoe when the dog had been just a gangling pup, to the epic five mile trek when she'd been 6, from the Hill to Lambourn, across the open gallops to the south with larks singing above, and frequent stops for sweets to keep her going.

Now Rosie leaned on the car and looked back into the sun, squinting her eyes at the lumpy outline of the hill fort's ramparts behind her, which somehow reminded her of Bill Grant's knuckles under her nose in the schoolyard. Beyond the fort's flank lay the thrilling but comforting thought of the Horse itself. But her father had turned it into – a job. She respected, she thought, her Dad's search, his effort, but sometimes it seemed to Rosie to miss the point.

It might be interesting that the lovely ripples of hillside along the Manger's edge had been caused by melting snow at the end of the Ice Age, and that they had been known locally as 'the Giant's Steps'. But sometimes, when Rosie looked at them, she felt the ripples in her stomach, and that was even more interesting. And there just behind them was the Horse, right there, right now, as real as when it had been thronged and fought over long ago. But her Dad – her Dad wanted to know what it had all meant.

Then, perhaps out of mild guilt for these slightly disloyal thoughts, Rosie decided to ask her father about the meaning of something that had been on her mind since that last talk with the motorcycle.

"Dad," she said, "you know Anneka has the transfers of those stacked-up rifles on her sides? And they made all those guns at the BSA factory? Yet we give her a girl's name, and when she's running she'll be for fun and excitement, nothing like killing and war. It just seems…"

"A contradiction?" said the Professor, his eyes sparkling. "But that's the way things have always been. Take the Horse. To the people then, horses and chariots were the cutting edge of war making. But horses were also much, much more to them than just fighting machines. They were beautiful; they meant speed, and fertility, crops and children growing healthy. Even when I was young, girls who wanted to have babies would stand in the eye of the Horse and wish for it. Maybe they still do! Wonderful herds of horses, multiplying all the time, that would have been how they measured the wealth of their tribes. Do you know what they would sometimes do? Strip off, paint themselves with blue woad, and race their horses sunwise, bareback, around the Hill, for the sheer joy of it!

"Horses for them meant the kind of power you feel inside yourself. They believed horses were associated with the sun – have you ever noticed that our White Horse was set running just about east to west, the same direction the sun rises and sets?" He paused, and tilted his head with his eyes half-closed, to let them both feel the sun on their faces. "What could be more life-giving than the sun, further away from death-bringing war? It was the same with the wheels on their chariots. The spoked wheel was a war symbol to them – but it was also a sun-symbol; it was round like the sun, and spokes radiated out from the centre like the rays of the sun." Rosie remembered Mike's talk of war, and the feel of the spokes of Anneka's wheel under her hands.

"So you see," her Dad finished, "maybe Anneka came out of war machines. Her forks were designed to be built on tools they had used to make gun barrels, which weren't going to be needed after the war. Yet when a motorbike is running well, nothing can make you feel more alive. So maybe it's the same way it was with these people. In their thinking, in their stories and pictures, they shifted their shapes, becoming part-human, part-animal. With these people, nothing is ever just one thing."

"Nothing is ever just one thing." The words echoed strangely in Rosie's head, she didn't know why.

After a moment, they climbed back into the car in companionable silence, grateful after the wind for the warm, still air inside. They drove along the narrow track westwards, clanked over another cattle grid, and turned right, downhill, past the car park, down the steep bumpy road off the Hill. Just before the crossroads at the bottom, the Professor pulled into a field-gate that gave a view back across the Manger to the Hill. It was one of the few spots from which you could see the White Horse virtually whole.

"Rosie, can you see how the sun on it makes it look different, clearer?" he asked. "I wanted to run a computer simulation of how the sun was aligned 3,000 years ago, to see if it helped explain why they put the Horse just there, where you can hardly see it…But the Team couldn't afford it, of course…"

Seeing him becoming despondent again, Rosie in turn got irritated. "Dad," she blurted out, "it's all in the *past*…"

"Yes," said her father mildly, "But there are lots of ways to bring the past alive again, Rosie. You can build up either actual things from it, like we're doing with Anneka, or a picture of how a whole place was, from a small part of it which you have – that's what we do at work, on an archaeological dig, and afterwards.

"You can try and make sense of the past that way. But maybe the best way of all is to do as much work on details like that as you can… and then fall into a dream, or take a leap of imagination, and put it all into a story. That's all the past is, all history is - a story. Or rather, lots of different stories, so you can take your pick. History – His-Story – or, Her-Story," he grinned, "if your mother has her way…"

"But you've always said we can't really know their stories," said Rosie, indicating the hill fort, "because they never wrote anything down."

"Ah, that's true," sighed the Professor. "But…not long ago, I started to hear rumours about a book, a book in Ireland. These people's priests had incredible memories, so they could learn their stories by heart, and remember them to hand them on from one generation to the next by word of mouth. Now in Ireland, there are several famous books, which came about when people could finally write these word-of-mouth stories down. They say that a man there has discovered another one. And the tale it tells has to do with a wonderful white horse, and a war between tribes in Ireland and England…

"Only they say that the man who has it is not at all keen to let anyone else see it. It would probably take more money than the Team could ever dream of, to persuade him. Anyway, it's only a rumour – just what they say…"

"Arr," said Rosie in a wonky country accent, "*they say*…" And the two of them drove off, laughing.

Then it was Half Term, and as they sometimes did, Rosie and her Mum, with Rosie's godmother Sue, went off to a holiday place for the week, leaving the Professor at home to work.

The holiday place mostly meant one thing to Rosie, and that was water. There were the big indoor pools under their high glass roof, planted round with palms. There was the "island", where the current swept streams of people round a narrow channel in a pleasant rush, so that you bobbed along feeling like a bath toy. There were the chutes and slides where you whizzed down a long steep ramp or a tunnel on a cushion of water, shrieking and hitting the pool at the bottom with a flat slap, before sinking to twist beneath the surface for long, disorienting moments, and then bursting up to the light again. And there were the outdoor hot pools, where you could lie flat, with warm water bubbling up all round your legs and back, pretending to be pasta or peas in a pan of boiling water.

It certainly beat school.

There were no cars, and they got everywhere, from the water place or the shops and restaurants to their hut in the pine forest, by bicycling, up and down wooden ramps and zigzag paths, under the tall trees. The huts were comfy, and when supper was over and it was bedtime, after she had said goodnight on the telephone to her father, Rosie liked to lie with her bedroom door ajar, and listen to the sound of her mother and Sue's voices as they shared a bottle of wine and talked quietly, before she drifted off to sleep. In the morning, right outside their big picture windows, she could watch the grey squirrels scampering up and down the misty tree trunks, and feeding from their forepaws.

The morning that they left the holiday place was a fine one, and as they got closer to the village, Rosie felt a rising sense of excitement at the thought of seeing home again, and all her things, and Zoe and her Dad.

When they turned into the drive, there was the black dog leaping up at the gate, desperate to greet them. And her father seemed almost as excited. While he hugged and kissed his wife and Rosie, he cried

"Perfect timing! Just you wait and see – come on!"

He led them round the corner to the shed. And there stood Anneka.

But not Anneka as they had known her. Now her bright red paint, lined with gold stripes, and her polished chrome,

sparkled in the sun. She sat confidently on her rebuilt wheels, with tyres so new that the little spikes of fresh rubber were still on them. Her tall wide handlebars were tilted at a jaunty angle, and the curving 'caterpillar' seat looked positively inviting. As a finishing touch, on her front mudguard was bolted the figure of the little winged silver lady, which her father had saved from his old BSA. Anneka looked a picture.

Rosie stood open-mouthed. She could hardly believe that this was the same rusting hulk that she had discovered in the barn. But it was.

"Mike the Bike came over to help and we worked on her every day," the Professor was babbling. "In fact we stayed up all one night to get her finished. She started second kick, and she runs wonderfully – I've ridden a couple of hundred miles on her already!"

But Rosie's eyes had fixed on a small, brand new, silver pilot-type helmet with goggles, which was resting on the seat. Mike had measured her for it before they went away. Only – had her father thrown the old helmet away? Would she still be able to hear Anneka? Then she spotted the old helmet safe inside the shed, standing on the orange tin tray with the cross-looking heron on it. So, relieved, she slipped on the new one. And got another shock.

" 'Allow ar kid," said the familiar downbeat voice. " 'Ow do oi look? Daont worry – oi can talk to yer through any crash-hat, long as it's been on me seat for a little while. Now, come on – 'ow do oi look?"

"*Beautiful*," thought Rosie. "*Amazing…*"

"Yeh, well, yer old man and that Moik did all roight by me. That Moik knows a bit. Yer father wanted to start me up roight away, but Moik med 'im turn me engine over with the kick start, till they could see the oil coming out of the pipe in the tank where it should do. And when he did start it, Moik put his finger over that pipe for a sec., to force the oil up the little pipes to wet me top end, me rockers. It's gorra be roit, eh? Now oi guz loik a bomb…"

Then her father was back beside her. He was wearing a thorn-proof jacket like Rosie's green one, only it was black, with a belt, and a high collar, and big brass snap-fasteners for its four outside pockets. He was also carrying a new silver helmet like Rosie's.

"Well my darling," he said, his eyes sparkling, "this is only fair, because it was you who found her. The first ride on the back is yours, if you want it. Your mother says it's all right with her – but only if you want to, of course…"

Rosie felt her heart pounding with excitement.

"Yes, please!" she said.

"Make sure you hold onto your father *tightly*, all the time," said her Mum who was smiling but looking a bit worried at the same time, as her father fastened the strap of Rosie's helmet under her chin.

"Wait while I start her," said her Dad, "and don't worry about the noise of the engine – it's only noise! Then hop on behind me – your mother will help, but don't stand on these passenger footrests while you're getting on, or they might break – wait till you're sitting on the saddle and then rest your feet on them. Keep your feet off the pipes, they get very hot. No singing – the bees fly into your mouth! And remember, hang onto me!"

The Professor straddled Anneka, pushed her off her stand with a clunk, pulled on the petrol tap under the tank, and fiddled with the carburettor. Then he pulled a lever on the handlebars, put his foot on the kick starter, and kicked.

Instantly the bike burst into life with a bellowing roar! Rosie couldn't help jumping back, as Zoe the dog went wild with excitement. But Rosie reminded herself "it's only noise," and very soon was enjoying the flat 'rumpetta-rumpetta' sound of Anneka's engine as it settled down.

" 'Ear me roar?" a voice chuckled in her ears. Then her father beckoned, and with her mother's help, in a moment Rosie was settling on the back of the comfy caterpillar seat, bathed in the noise, her hands clasped round her Dad's waist and her helmetted head pressed against his back as her heart pounded. She felt her Dad's right leg move and the bike lurch slightly as his foot clicked the lever up into first gear, and then smoothly they began to move.

They rolled forward over the squirming gravel, and through the garden gate. At the front gate they halted for a moment to check the road each way for traffic, then her father said "Are you OK?" and when Rosie shouted "Yes!" they moved off again, turning right to set off down the solid, sunlit road.

There was a moment of nervousness, as they picked up speed and changed gear once, and then again. But after that Rosie found herself revelling in the ride, the roaring engine and the feel of the wind on her face as they sped forward, with Anneka a powerful living thing beneath them. Her father glanced over his right shoulder to check for traffic behind, so to keep out of his way Rosie peered round his left side, watching the hedges and cow parsley whizzing by, and the first set of bends coming up fast.

That was another moment, when her Dad tilted the bike left for the first time and the whole earth seemed to tilt with it. But Rosie fought the urge to stay upright, leaned over just as her father did, and loved the way they swung through the curve, and then smoothly pulled upright again and in one supple movement were swinging over the other way, as the next bend followed the first. Her tummy felt funny, but only for a moment, and then she was into the ride, into the road, leaning further for the tight right hand bend before the long straight bit, where her father changed up again and they flew for half a mile down the middle of the unwavering road towards the big village, Anneka's springs soaking up the bumps, tears from the wind streaming down Rosie's face till she remembered to pull her goggles down over her eyes.

"Go on, Dad," she found herself shouting, "Go faster!" and she saw her father glance back with a smile and felt the BSA pulling harder for a moment, before they were coming to the right turn before the village, and the throttle blipped once, twice, as her father down-shifted, heeled the bike all the way over and pulled smoothly away again, going up through the gears.

"I love this!" yelled Rosie aloud at the top of her voice, before she remembered about the bees. And she did love it, settling down to drink in the sound of the wind rushing by, to feel the engine's deep song in her chest, and savour the whole roaring glory of the ride. They bumped up and over a long uneven hump in the road where the old canal ran under it, her father standing up slightly on his footpegs the same way she would rise to the trot in her stirrups on a pony. They rode past the Mushroom Woods, where the thick trees close by the roadside threw back the roar of the engine louder, and snaked over the narrow railway bridge and round the bend, to where the road ran alongside the railway tracks. Suddenly Rosie felt her head duck down into her collar instinctively, as without warning, a two-carriage train whooshed past them from behind, but her Dad shouted "Wave!" as he speeded up, and she did, and thought she saw someone from the blurred train waving back.

Then as the road peeled away from the railway they were tilting hard left for a long, long curve, Rosie feeling the tension as Anneka's rear wheel wanted to break away on the gravelled road, but the right speed, their weight and the BSA's steady roadholding kept them on track. They slowed at a crossroads for a hard turn right, bumped along an even narrower lane, and then shot downwards into the shadows beneath the narrow railway bridge where for a split second the engine noise racketed back in a deafening echo from the brick arch, before they zoomed out again into the sunlight.

Sharp bends past a couple of farm entrances, and then they were on another long, flat, empty stretch. "Faster!" yelled Rosie, but her Dad shouted something she couldn't hear, which turned out to be "Her engine's still running in!" though he did hold on a little in 3rd gear before they snicked into top, rocketing along beside woods and fields, where bay horses pricked their ears and startled black crows lifted desperately at the thundering noise.

Her father was riding more confidently now, and Rosie was pushed into his back after he had held their speed and then braked hard, down-changed and leaned sharp left as the bike lifted on its springs taking another hump in the road, and immediately jinked hard left and then right, with a hint of a skid from the back wheel, before they were starting up the first slope of the climb, where the road rose to the village above the one where they lived.

Anneka pulled powerfully, easily, up the long steep hill, and then in tree-shadow they levelled off, slowed, and entered the village. Outside the first row of houses, Rosie saw Mrs Wilsden, the kind lady who helped at their cottage, working in her garden. Mrs Wilsden straightened to squint at the noise of the bike, and then her eyes widened and her mouth dropped open as she recognised Rosie, and they waved frantically at each other. Past the pub, past the little church where Rosie had been christened, and then they were waiting at the junction for a silver car to pass, and turning right, followed the car steadily down the curve of the hill and back into their own village.

As they approached their front gate, her father yelled "Want to go on?" and when Rosie shouted "Yes!" they both waved wildly at her Mum standing on the drive who finally smiled and gestured for them to go on, when she saw what a good time they were having.

They rode back the way they had started, only this time they slowed and kept straight on into the big village where Rosie went to school. She was delighted to spot her friend Ernest, and Bill Grant, roller-blading at the rec., and watch their heads come up at the sound of the BSA and their jaws drop as they realised who it was behind the goggles, waving at them from the back. They rode past the school and the tall church, then turned right carefully over mounds of gravel on the corner. They tilted round the high verges of the bend where Rosie's Dad always told them that his mother, before the war, had run over a hen in her Bull-nose Morris car. She had had to pay the people 5 shillings for the hen, but they had let her keep the egg it had laid in *rigor mortis*.

They thundered out of the village, up and over another long hump in the road where the canal had run, and then cruised down a straight stretch between fields towards the tunnel under another, larger railway bridge. They rode through it with an echoing roar again, and as they drove on through bends and started uphill, Rosie realised that she had rarely felt as happy as she did at that moment. They were all one – her, her father, the bike and the road. It was as if the motorbike had been designed just for this, these winding country roads; steering so surely, its sound exciting but steady, not too fast, but certainly not too slow! It might be a different story in the rain, but this was a perfect day, bright, sunny and clear, a day when larks would soar and sing, and your thoughts could travel a thousand miles in an instant.

Then at the top of the hill, on the second, sharp bend, she realised that her father was slowing to a halt. Beneath a stag-headed oak tree, there was the broad entrance to a rutted farm

track down a lane, and the Professor turned the bike in there, bumping them round in a half-circle with his feet still up on the rests and bringing them to a dusty halt in the shade, facing back towards the village, and rising beyond it, White Horse Hill.

Her father killed the engine. In the ringing silence, a hesitant voice in Rosie's ears said

"D'you loike it, then?"

"*Oh, yes!*" thought Rosie. Anneka was remarking that her Dad wasn't a bad rider, 'firm, but not 'ard,' when the Professor said

"We always used to bicycle up here when I was a kid. My Mum would give me and Tom Ellis, my pal from the village, picnic lunches, and pack us off, and this is where we'd usually come. It's a good view of the Hill, and if we pushed our bikes into the field there, under the hedge, it was a sheltered spot. In fact, the old gypsies sometimes used to pull their caravans and horses in there."

"And did you used to stay all day?" asked Rosie, climbing off the bike, being careful to avoid the hot silencers.

"No, we'd eat everything and be back before lunch," laughed her Dad. "It used to drive my mother mad..."

Then they stood in silence, Rosie still wearing her helmet. And gradually she realised that there was a stillness in her, a stillness in particular contrast to the speed and noise of the ride. In the ringing silence, something inside her trembled, just as it had, she thought, in those moments before she had entered the barn and found Anneka. Something was going to happen. Was it, she thought? Well, if it was, it was.

They stood looking out over the railway line, the village and the tall eight-sided tower of "the Cathedral of the Vale", to the Hill rising beyond. It was an exceptionally clear day, and they could plainly see, against the green slopes, bits of the White Horse. Only the lie of the slopes meant that from this side, all you could see were three white strokes, portions of the whole. And now they reminded Rosie of something. But not a horse...

"Looks loik a bird," said the voice in her ear. "Sroit thou, intit?"

And then Rosie realised just what she had been reminded of by the shape in the distance. It was the bad-tempered heron on that old tin tray in the shed. And as she realised that, other things flooded her mind all at once. Her father's words on the Hill:

"For these people, nothing is ever just one thing…" And that morning at school, learning about the man who had painted things that were more than one thing at once. Like the insides of a well-oiled lock when the right key is turned, in Rosie's mind everything clicked absolutely into place.

Almost painfully, she looked up at her father and said "Dad..?"

And perhaps because she had been away for a week, and because he was feeling so happy to have her back, and happy with the way all their work on the bike had paid off, the Professor said

"Yes, my darling?" and then really listened to what she had to say.

"Dad, when you look at the Horse from here, it looks like a bird, doesn't it? Sort of like a heron or something?"

"Yes, yes I suppose it does," said her father.

"And you know how you're always bothered by how you can't really see the whole Horse? Well…supposing you weren't meant to all the time? Supposing that from one direction, like here, it was a bird? After all, it has a bird's head. And from another direction, from the Manger, it was a Horse. Dad, supposing it was *meant to be both*."

There was a long silence, and during it her father's expression slowly changed. Then he spoke, hoarsely.

"Herons…wading birds…*cranes*! Rosie, you're a genius! There was always an association of wading birds with horses in their religion," he babbled, "on several of their coins the two are figured together. We know it was a widespread idea, an important idea to them. And there it is, under our noses all the time, and nobody sees it, none of us – till *you*, now!" He grabbed Rosie and hugged her, so that the helmet clonked on his chest.

"This could be a really important breakthrough," he told her eagerly. "Apart from anything else, it opens the way to the Irish connection - cranes were common in the Irish tales. And only an Irishman would have had the bare-faced cheek, three thousand years ago, to draw a picture with a trick like that in it – one thing from one way and one from another – and to make it 125 feet tall!

"And cranes always had female connections, in the stories they were always transformed women, never men. But the sun-horse, that was a male thing. A picture that combined, and maybe reconciled, the two – no wonder we still feel the pull of it…Come on," he cried, tugging on his helmet excitedly, "we have to get back and talk to some people. This is going to change a lot of things, Rosie, change them for the better. Funding, maybe a book, all that…and it's all because of you, Rosie, you and your sharp eyes, my darling!"

"It was Anneka, really," said Rosie, and then blushed scarlet as her father raised his eyebrows in surprise. "I mean, if she hadn't taken us up to this spot, today…"

"*That's roight*," came the gloomy voice in her ear, "*give credit where it's due…*"

A week later, Lorna Honeywell stood outside the farmhouse, shading her eyes with one hand against the afternoon sun.

Behind her, the farm tearoom was decorated with flowers and balloons, and full of people. The Ransoms had hired it for that Saturday afternoon, and invited Rosie's friends Ernest and Anna with their parents, and Mike the Bike with his wife and family, as well Mrs Wisden and her husband, and the Professor's friends from the Oxford Archaeological Team.

The new theory about the Horse had revived the Team's fortunes. There had been immediate, intense interest from the newspapers and television about this radical new thinking on such a well known and well loved landmark. Generous funding for further research was a virtual certainty, with all the publicity. In fact there was a TV crew waiting now outside the tearoom to interview the Professor and Rosie, for her father had made no secret of the role his daughter and Anneka the motorbike had played in the breakthrough.

But Mrs Honeywell was worried. Her guests of honour still had not arrived.

Then she heard the faint roar of a powerful engine. The noise on the road below grew louder, and soon she heard it gun down through the gears and turn into the farm lane. The note of the engine changed as it pulled hard up the hill, and above that

there came the sound of shouting. Then the red motorbike burst into view, its passengers yelling their heads off, and skidded to a halt by the farm's front door.

Mrs Honeywell's big brown eyes were almost out on stalks.

"What do you think you look like?" she gasped, as the TV camera crew pressed forward while the Professor and Rosie, who were covered in white dust, tugged off their helmets and sat on the bike laughing – their faces striped with bright blue paint!

"It's what they used to do to celebrate in the old days," cried Rosie, "paint themselves with woad and ride sun-wise round the Hill! And that's what we've just done!"

The ride had had its moments, starting with the steep, steep pull up Blowing Stone Hill, then turning onto the Ridgeway track, its mud surface baked hard by the weeks of fine weather. They had bumped along between the hedges by the Gallops, past a tall copse of trees and then up the long rise beside Mrs Honeywell's top fields, climbing towards the very crest of the Ridgeway. Often the deep ruts tried to trap their wheels and force them one way, but Rosie clung on as the Professor steered Anneka free along the bumpy grass verges, and soon they were sailing along the top behind the hill fort, Rosie waving at the walkers they met. Some of them had looked startled, or cross, at the noisy red motorbike and its blue-faced riders, but others knew the Ransoms or recognised Anneka from the pictures in the local papers, and they had waved back, beaming.

Then came the most frightening bit of the ride, as they started down the long chalk slope of the Ridgeway from the top of the Hill, where really deep, slippery, white chalk gullies insisted on how they went, and there was nothing to do but hang on, leave the brakes alone, and trust Anneka. A cloud of white dust rose in their wake as the rear wheel slipped and skidded, and the bouncing meant that Rosie's bottom seemed to spend more time in the air than on the caterpillar saddle. But eventually they were safely down, and turned right at the bottom to reach pot-holed tarmac, ride past the

74

car park and down more steep hill, then right, onto the road again, with the Horse glittering in the sun up to their right as they plunged down, round, up again, past the cross-roads and finally into the farm entrance.

"Park the bike over there in the barn," said Mrs Honeywell, "and come and say hello to everybody. And then I want my go on the pillion, Professor!" Rosie's Dad nodded, smiling, snicked into gear and drove over to an open wooden barn. Inside, the farm's original Land Rover lay in pieces, where Mrs Honeywell's oldest son was restoring it.

As the Professor drove into the barn and cut the engine, Anneka's wondering voice sounded in Rosie's ears.

"Oider now, ar kid, this is stringe. Oi niver thought oi'd be back 'ere! This barn, this was where oi lived, all them years ago…It's loik coming home again…"

"*Will you be all right?*" thought Rosie gently.

"Oh aye," said the voice cheerfully. "Oimagunna talk to this Land Rowver. 'E's even older than oi am! Both made in Brumigem, we wuz," said Anneka proudly.

Rosie slipped off her helmet again, patted the BSA's seat and walked away. Mike the Bike was limping across the yard to her Dad with a mug of tea in his hand, grinning broadly.

"Go all right, did she, Ace?" he called.

"She's a peach," said the Professor enthusiastically. "I say, will you check her over towards the end of next week? Thanks to all this," he gestured at the camera crew, "we'll be able to take a proper holiday for the first time in a couple of years. We're going to the place we like in the South of France. The girls will fly down, but I'm going to ride there on Anneka!"

"Don't worry," said Mike, "I'll give 'er a proper going over. She'll do good…"

Rosie waved at Anna and Ernest, as she watched her mother crossing the yard from the farm kitchen carrying a baking tray of fresh scones. With butter, cream and homemade strawberry

jam, she and her friends were in for a feast. Life was good.

And after the party was all over, and the people had gone, her father had promised her a ride on Anneka back up to the Horse. Perhaps she would walk to the Eye under the rising moon, and make a wish. Her usual wish, she thought. With what they had discovered, it seemed especially right.

To fly.